LIGHT

By
Steffi Cavell-Clarke

Published in 2017 by
KidHaven Publishing, an Imprint of Greenhaven Publishing, LLC
353 3rd Avenue
Suite 255
New York, NY 10010

Designer: Danielle Jones
Editor: Grace Jones

Cataloging-in-Publication Data

Names: Cavell-Clarke, Steffi.
Title: Light / Steffi Cavell-Clarke.
Description: New York : KidHaven Publishing, 2017. | Series: First science | Includes index.
Identifiers: ISBN 9781534520721 (pbk.) | ISBN 9781534520745 (library bound) | ISBN 9781534520738 (6 pack) | ISBN 9781534520752 (ebook)
Subjects: LCSH: Light–Juvenile literature. | Shades and shadows–Juvenile literature. | Reflection (Optics)–Juvenile literature.
Classification: LCC QC360.C38 2017 | DDC 535–dc23

Printed in the United States of America

CPSIA compliance information: Batch #CW17KL: For further information contact Greenhaven Publishing LLC, New York, New York at 1-844-317-7404.

Please visit our website, www.greenhavenpublishing.com. For a free color catalog of all our high-quality books, call toll free 1-844-317-7404 or fax 1-844-317-7405.

PHOTO CREDITS

Abbreviations: l-left, r-right, b-bottom, t-top, c-center, m-middle.

Front cover – Jenn Huls. 2 – Sergey Novikov. 4 – Brian A Jackson. 5 – Tom Wang. 6 – Andrey Arkusha. 7 – Anna Jurkovska. 8 – vvita. 9l – ILYA GENKIN. 9m – Moises Fernandez Acosta. 9r – wenani. 9rb Hard Ligth. 10 – Gelpi JM. 11 – mik ulyannikov. 12 – Boris Mrdja. 13 – Djem. 14 – Alexey Repka. 15 – enn Huls. 16 – Pablo77. 17 – Pavel Kriuchkov. 18 – SuriyaPhoto. 19 – Wingedbull. 20 – Soloviova Liudmyla. 21 – Galyna Andrushko. 22l – CPM PHOTO. 22r – StockPhotosArt. 23 – Johanna Altmann. Images are courtesy of Shutterstock.com. With thanks to Getty Images, Thinkstock Photo, and iStockphoto.

CONTENTS

Words that look like **this** can be found in the glossary on page 24.

What Is
SCIENCE?

Where does light come from?

What helps us see all the colors in a rainbow?

Why are we unable to see in the dark?

Science can answer many difficult questions we may have and help us understand the world around us.

What Is LIGHT?

Light is very important because it helps us see all the things and people around us.

When there is no light, it is dark.
We cannot see in the dark.

7

Where Does **LIGHT** Come From?

Light can come from many different places. These are called light sources.

Flashlights, lamps, and lighthouses are all light sources. Our biggest light source is the sun.

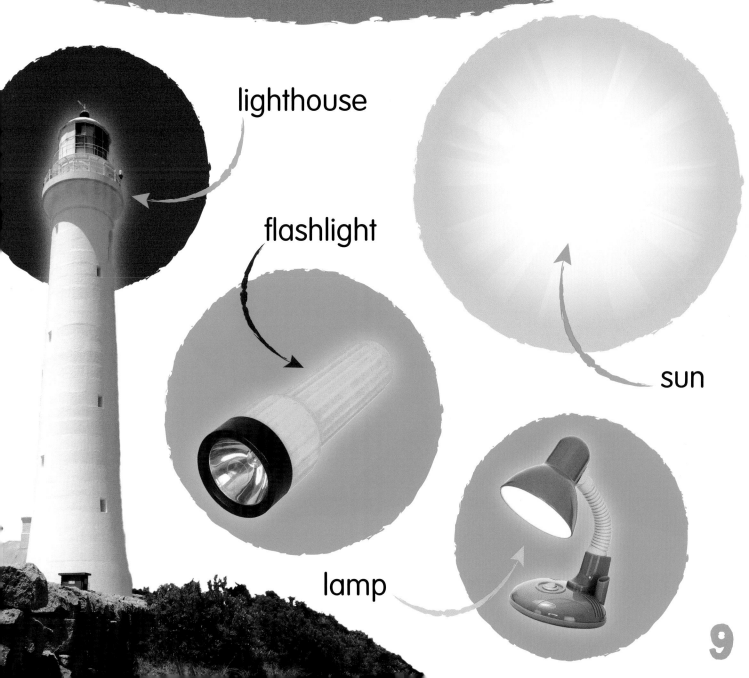

lighthouse

flashlight

sun

lamp

How Does LIGHT MOVE?

Light moves from its source in **waves**.
The waves move in straight lines.

Light is always moving. The **speed** of light is very fast. It is the fastest moving thing on Earth.

We should never look directly at the sun because it might damage our eyes.

11

How Do We SEE?

pupil

People and animals need light to see. Your eyes take in light through your **pupils**.

A special part of your eye, which is called the lens, makes a picture from the light and sends it to your brain.

lens

What Is SUNLIGHT?

The sun is a **star** that gives Earth light and warmth.
Every living thing on Earth needs sunlight.

Sunlight allows people and animals to see during the day. Plants also need sunlight to grow.

What Is ELECTRICITY?

Electricity is used to make light. Electricity is a type of **energy** that has many different uses.

You can use electricity to switch on electric lights at home when it is dark.

What Are

green

red

blue

We can see many different colors.
What colors can you see around you?

Light is made up of different colors. When light waves travel through rain, it shows all the light's colors.

This is called a rainbow.

19

What Are SHADOWS?

shadow

Light waves cannot bend or go around corners.
When an object or a person blocks the light
waves, a shadow is made.

Many shadows are cast throughout the day. Houses, cars, and trees can cause shadows by blocking the sunlight.

Let's
EXPERIMENT!

Do you know how to make a shadow?
Let's find out!

STEP 1

Make a shadow puppet by asking
an adult to cut out a shape from the paper.
Attach the shape to the straw with tape.

STEP 2

Switch the flashlight on and place it on a table facing
a wall or sheet.

STEP 3

Hold the puppet between the flashlight and the wall. Can you see the shadow it makes?

TOP TIP:
Ask an adult to help you!

RESULTS:

You should be able to see how light shines from its source and casts a shadow when it is blocked.

23

GLOSSARY

energy   power used to do an activity

pupils   special parts of the eye that let light in

sources   where something comes from

speed   how fast something moves

star   a giant ball of hot gas in space

waves   a kind of movement that transfers energy from place to place

INDEX

24